ed vere

HOW TO BE A
LION

The world is full of ideas.

Big ones,
small ones.
Good ones,
bad ones.

Some think this . . .
              others think that.

Some say,
    there's only **one** way to be a lion.

                            They say . . .

Lions are FIERCE!

If they catch you,
    they will chomp you.

Crunch,

    crunch,

        CHOMP!

They say a lion can't be gentle.

Well, *they* haven't met Leonard.

Leonard loves to walk by himself,
feeling the sun warm his back
and the grass under his paws.

Some days, Leonard walks to his thinking hill.

Sometimes he thinks important thoughts . . .
Sometimes he daydreams.

Somewhere in between,
he hums quietly and plays with words.
Putting them together
this way, then that way—
making them into poems.

Some say,

WAIT!

Lions are **not** gentle!

Lions do **not** write poems!

And if a lion met a duck . . .

Bad luck for that duck.

Crunch,

crunch,

CHOMP!

But if Leonard met a duck . . .

What do **you** think would happen?

"Hello," said Leonard. "I'm Leonard."

"Hello," said the duck. "I'm Marianne."

"I'm writing a poem," said Leonard,
"but I'm stuck. Will you help me?"

"You're in luck," said Marianne.
"I'm a poetic duck."

Together,
they played with Leonard's poem,
until the words came unstuck.

Leonard and Marianne found they liked each other.

Under the sun, in the long grass, they lay together.

They played.

They went for walks
and had long meandering conversations,
    a mixture of quacks and quiet roars.

At night they watched for shooting stars,
and made wishes if they saw them.

"Do you think the universe has edges?"
quacked Marianne.

"If it doesn't," said Leonard,
"will we fall out?"

Together, they are happy.
They wish for nothing more than this.

(Some say that a lion should have chomped a duck by now . . .)

One day a pack of fierce lions came
prowling around.

"What's going on here?" they growled.
"Why hasn't this duck
been chomped?"

"This duck is Marianne," said Leonard.
"She's my friend and nobody will chomp her!"

The fierce lions came closer.

"We heard you're gentle.
We heard you make up poems.
But not chomping a duck?
                    You've gone **too** far!"

The fierce lions growled and roared . . .

"There's only **one** way to be a lion . . .

Leonard,
you **must** be fierce!"

"Must I be fierce?"
said Leonard.
            "Must I change?"

"They're wrong!" quacked Marianne.
            "And we will show them why."

Leonard and Marianne went to their thinking hill.
They thought hard.

After a while Leonard hummed a serious hum.
An idea started to form.

Marianne quacked a serious quack.
The idea grew.

They put their words together,
like this, like that, building them into a poem
        that made sense of what they thought.

Finally they were ready.

Leonard took a deep breath . . .

"I'll say this quietly,
I needn't roar to be heard,
I can be a friend
to a bee or a bird.

You said I must change, I must chomp Marianne,
but chomping your friends is a terrible plan.

Let nobody say
just **one** way is true.
There are so many ways
that you can be you.

If there **must** be a must,
then this we must try . . .

Why don't you, be **you** . . .

And I, will be **I**."

Some say words can't change the world.
Leonard says, if they make you think,
then maybe they can.

Is there just **one** way to be a lion?

I don't think so . . .

Do you?

This book is for those who daydream,
and those who think for themselves.

With thanks to Andrea MacDonald, Goldy Broad and Frances Gilbert.
And to Sophie Darlington for a place to stay full of inspiration.

All rights reserved. Published in the United States by Doubleday,
an imprint of Random House Children's Books, a division of Penguin Random House LLC, New York.
Simultaneously published in the United Kingdom by Puffin Books, London, in 2018.
Doubleday and the colophon are registered trademarks of Penguin Random House LLC.

Visit us on the Web! rhcbooks.com
Educators and librarians, for a variety of teaching tools, visit us at RHTeachersLibrarians.com

Library of Congress Cataloging-in-Publication Data
Names: Vere, Ed, author, illustrator.
Title: How to be a lion / Ed Vere.
Description: First American edition. | New York : Doubleday, 2018. | Summary: "When Leonard the lion and his friend Marianne,
a duck, are confronted by a pack of lion bullies, they find a creative way to stand up for themselves." —Provided by publisher.
Identifiers: LCCN 2017038326 (print) | LCCN 2017048236 (ebook) | ISBN 978-0-525-57805-5 (trade) |
ISBN 978-0-525-57806-2 (library binding) | ISBN 978-0-525-57807-9 (ebook)
Subjects: | CYAC: Individuality—Fiction. | Lions—Fiction. | Ducks—Fiction. | Bullies—Fiction. | Friendship—Fiction. | Poetry—Fiction.
Classification: LCC PZ7.V586 (ebook) | LCC PZ7.V586 How 2018 (print) | DDC [E]—dc23

MANUFACTURED IN CHINA
10 9 8 7 6 5 4 3 2 1   First American Edition
Random House Children's Books supports the First Amendment and celebrates the right to read.

Doubleday Books for Young Readers

Lions are endangered. You can help them here:
www.ruahacarnivoreproject.com & www.lionguardians.org
Thank you!

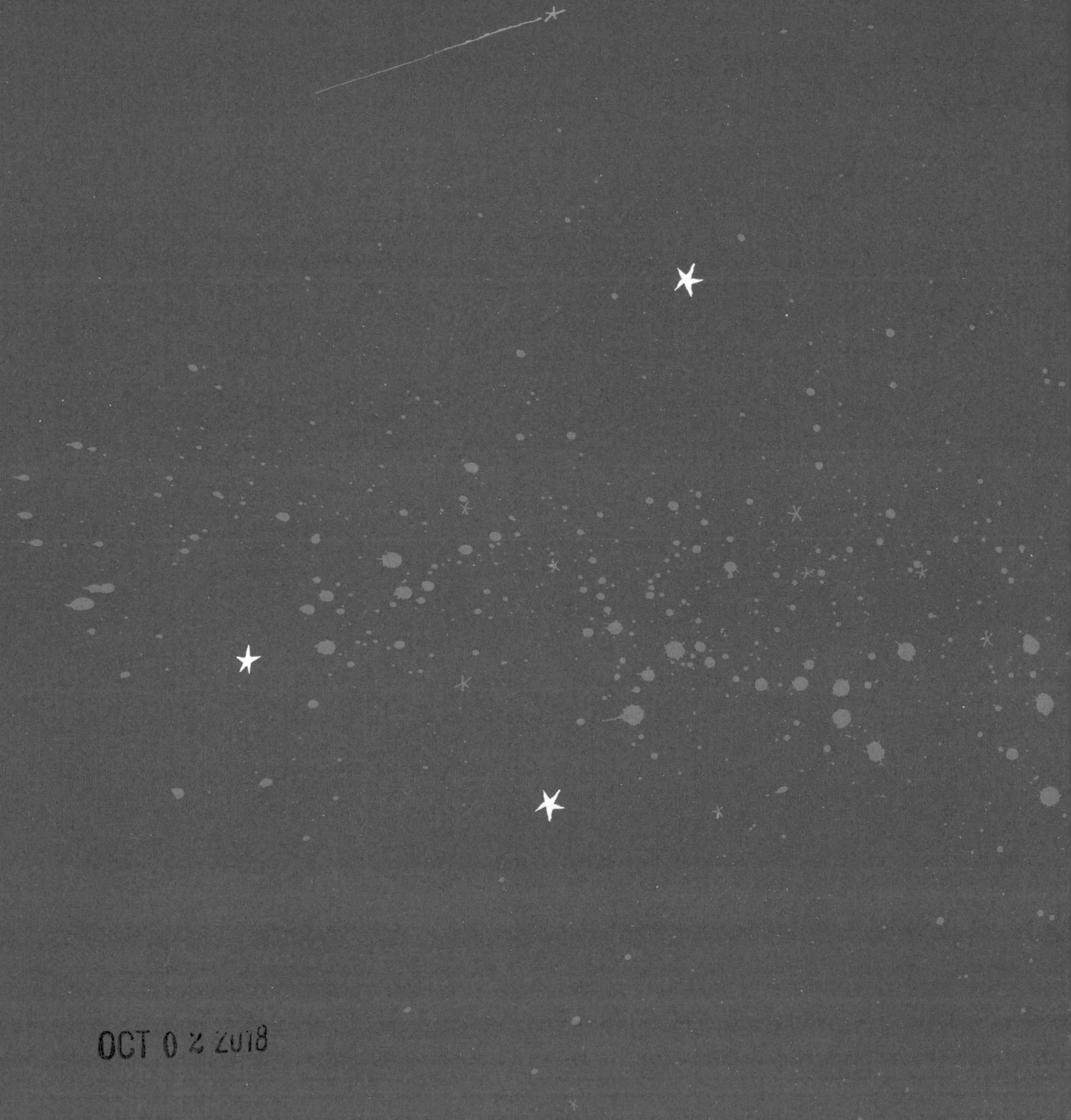